Rise and Shine, Mariko-chan!

by Chiyoko Tomioka
Illustrated by Yoshiharu Tsuchida

SCHOLASTIC INC.
New York Toronto London Auckland Sydney

"Rise and shine, Mariko-chan!" Mariko hears her mother calling.

She stretches wide and gets out of bed.

Her mother is making
breakfast in the kitchen.
"Good morning, Mariko-
chan. Are you awake yet?"
"I think so, Mama," says
Mariko.

On the table, Mariko sees some tomato, egg, and cucumber.

"Mama, it looks like a traffic light!" she says.

Mama laughs. "Mariko-chan, go wash your face before we eat."

Mariko washes up in the bathroom with her big sister, Yuko.

"Yuko, will you always be bigger than me?" Mariko asks.

"Yes," says Yuko.

"Will you always be bigger than Yumi?"

"Yes," says Yuko. "And even if you both grow bigger than me, I'll always be the oldest sister. That's why I think oldest is best."

"I think littlest is best," says Mariko.

"Mariko-chan,"
Mama calls, "it's time
to get dressed."
Mariko wants to
wear her favorite shirt
with the bear on it,
but it's still on the
clothesline. She picks
out her other favorite
shirt, the one with
cherries.

"Mama, Yuko says oldest is best," says Mariko.

"For her, it *is* the best," says Mama.

"Is littlest the best, too?"

"Yes, Mariko-chan," says Mama.

"But what about Yumi?" asks Mariko.

"For Yumi, middle is best," says Mama.
"Hold still for a moment, please."

Now it's time for breakfast.
Mariko is happy — Mama
has made rice balls. She
can hardly wait to start
eating.

But Yumi, Mariko's middle
sister, is not happy. "I don't
want to eat my rice ball,"
she says.

"I'll eat it!" cries Mariko.

"Mariko-chan loves
rice balls," says Daddy.
"That's why she has
such big round cheeks!"

"If I loved tomatoes,"
she asks, "would I have
big red eyes?"

"No, Mariko-chan,"
says Oba-san, Mariko's
grandmother. "You
would have pretty black
eyes, just like you have
now."

After breakfast, Yuko and Yumi are very busy getting ready for school. Mariko plays with her bear and watches them run back and forth through the house.

"Where are my notebooks?" shouts Yuko.

"Where is my pencil case?" cries Yumi.

When Yuko and Yumi are finally ready to leave, Mariko stands by the door. Every morning, Mariko and her sisters like to shake hands.

"Good-bye," says Yuko.
"See you after school, Mariko-chan!" says Yumi.
"Bye!" says Mariko. "See you after school!"

"Now it's your turn," says Mama.

Mama brushes Mariko's hair until it's shiny and neat.

She helps Mariko put on her blue jacket, and then places her yellow school bag over her shoulder.

Then she sets Mariko's hat carefully on her head.

"Now you're all ready for school, too," says Mama. "And now it's my turn to get ready for work."

Daddy calls to Mama, "Are you ready to go?" Every morning Mama and Daddy go to work together in the car.

Finally Mama and Daddy are ready to leave. They
say good-bye to Oba-san at the door. Mariko carries
Daddy's briefcase out to the car.

"Good-bye, Mariko-chan," says Mama. "Have a good day at school."

"Will you bring home some strawberries?" Mariko asks.

"Yes, on the way home," says Mama.

"Promise? Promise?" cries Mariko.

They link their pinkie fingers together and shake. "I promise, promise, double promise," says Mama. "Good-bye, Mariko-chan!"

Out in the yard, Mariko waits for the yellow school bus with Oba-san.

"Is it coming yet?" she asks.

Oba-san looks up the street. "Not yet, Mariko-chan."

"Is it coming *yet*?" Mariko asks.

Oba-san looks again. "Not yet."

"Oba-san, is it coming *now*?"

Oba-san looks one more time. "Yes, now it's coming."

"Hooray!"

Mariko runs to the bus, singing a little song. "Good morning, good morning, good mor-r-rning!"

"Good morning, Mariko!" calls the bus driver.

Mariko climbs on the bus with all her friends. Then she waves to Oba-san.

"See you after school, Oba-san," she says.

"Good-bye, Mariko-chan," says Oba-san.

And the yellow school bus takes Mariko to school.

A Note to the Reader:

The family in this story is Japanese. Their names are pronounced this way:

Mariko: *Mah-ree-ko*

Yuko: *Yoo-ko*

Yumi: *Yoo-mee*

Oba-san: *Oh-baah-san*

In Japanese, "chan" and "san" are added to the end of a name to show affection and respect. "Chan" is used especially for children and close friends, and "san" is used for adults and family elders. In this book, "Mariko-chan" means "little Mariko" or "Mariko dear." "Oba-san" means "dear Grandmother" or "Grandma."

The hand-formed, triangular-shaped rice balls that Mama prepares are called onigiri (*oh-nee-gee-ree*).

One Japanese custom for sealing a promise is to link pinkie fingers, shake them, and sing, "Yubikiri genman uso tsuitara hari sen bon nomasu" (*yoo-bee-kee-ree gen-man oo-so tsoo-ee-tah-rah ha-ree sen bohn no-mah-soo*). In this book, the phrase was adapted to, "I promise, promise, double promise." The expression actually means, "I promise, you promise, who breaks this promise must swallow a thousand needles."

Previously published in Japan as *Chiko-chan, Itterasshai (See You Later, Chiko-chan)*.

Text copyright © 1986 by Chiyoko Tomioka.
English text copyright © 1992 by Scholastic Inc.
Illustrations copyright © 1986 by Yoshiharu Tsuchida.
All rights reserved. Published by Scholastic Inc., 730 Broadway, New York, NY 10003,
by arrangement with Fukutake Publishing Company, Ltd. English adaptation by Lauren Stevens,
based on translations by Cathy Hirano and Jennifer Riggs.

Library of Congress Cataloging-in-Publication Data

Tomioka, Chiyoko.
 [Chiko-chan, Itterasshai. English]
 Rise and shine, Mariko-chan! / by Chiyoko Tomioka : illustrated by
Yoshiharu Tsuchida.
  p. cm.
 Translation of: Chiko-chan, Itterasshai.
 Summary: The youngest of three sisters in a Japanese family gets
ready for a day at preschool.
 ISBN 0-590-45507-9
 [1. Japan—Fiction. 2. Family life—Fiction.] I. Tsuchida,
Yoshiharu, ill. II. Title
PZ7.T5846Ri   1992
[E]—dc20   92-7897
                                                                   CIP
                                                                   AC

12 11 10 9 8 7 6 5 4 3 2 1   2 3 4 5 6 7/9

Printed in the U.S.A.   08

First Scholastic printing, August 1992